Dear Parents:

Congratulations! Your child is taking the first steps on an exciting journey. The destination? Independent reading!

STEP INTO READING® will help your child get there. The program offers five steps to reading success. Each step includes fun stories and colorful art or photographs. In addition to original fiction and books with favorite characters, there are Step into Reading Non-Fiction Readers, Phonics Readers and Boxed Sets, Sticker Readers, and Comic Readers—a complete literacy program with something to interest every child.

Learning to Read, Step by Step!

Ready to Read   Preschool–Kindergarten
• big type and easy words • rhyme and rhythm • picture clues
For children who know the alphabet and are eager to begin reading.

Reading with Help   Preschool–Grade 1
• basic vocabulary • short sentences • simple stories
For children who recognize familiar words and sound out new words with help.

Reading on Your Own   Grades 1–3
• engaging characters • easy-to-follow plots • popular topics
For children who are ready to read on their own.

Reading Paragraphs   Grades 2–3
• challenging vocabulary • short paragraphs • exciting stories
For newly independent readers who read simple sentences with confidence.

Ready for Chapters   Grades 2–4
• chapters • longer paragraphs • full-color art
For children who want to take the plunge into chapter books but still like colorful pictures.

STEP INTO READING® is designed to give every child a successful reading experience. The grade levels are only guides; children will progress through the steps at their own speed, developing confidence in their reading.

Remember, a lifetime love of reading starts with a single step!

For Rachel, my superhero sister
—L.E.

Copyright © 2023 DC. WONDER WOMAN and all related characters and elements ™ & © DC. WB SHIELD: ™ & © Warner Bros. Entertainment Inc. (s23)

Published in the United States by Random House Children's Books, a division of Penguin Random House LLC, 1745 Broadway, New York, NY 10019, and in Canada by Penguin Random House Canada Limited, Toronto.

Step into Reading, Random House, and the Random House colophon are registered trademarks of Penguin Random House LLC.

Visit us on the Web!
StepIntoReading.com
rhcbooks.com

Educators and librarians, for a variety of teaching tools, visit us at RHTeachersLibrarians.com

ISBN 978-0-593-57111-8 (trade) — ISBN 978-0-593-57112-5 (lib. bdg.)
ISBN 978-0-593-57113-2 (ebook)

Printed in the United States of America

10 9 8 7 6 5 4 3 2 1

Random House Children's Books supports the First Amendment and celebrates the right to read.

WONDER WOMAN™
Sisters Save the Day!

by Lois Evans

illustrated by Melissa Manwill

Wonder Woman created by
William Moulton Marston

Random House 🏠 New York

4

Wonder Woman loves
her sister, Nubia.
They live on
Paradise Island.
They train together
to be warriors.
The sisters are always
ready for action!

The Undersea Games
are in Atlantis.
The queen asks
Wonder Woman
and Nubia to represent
Paradise Island.

The sisters are excited to go to Atlantis!

7

In Atlantis they meet
Princess Mera.
She is a kind leader.
Mera has a twin sister
named Siren.

Siren is not
at the games.

The three girls see
all the other players.
Then a big octopus
suddenly appears!
It grabs one
of them!

Siren is riding on
the octopus.
She is angry.
She wants to take over
the games!

Mera, Wonder Woman,
and Nubia

spring into action.

Nubia and her sister
take the children
to safety.

The sisters swim back
to help Mera.

Mera and some sailfish
swim around and around
the octopus,
forming a whirlpool.
They stop the octopus!

Unlike Wonder Woman
and Nubia, Siren
and Mera do not
get along.

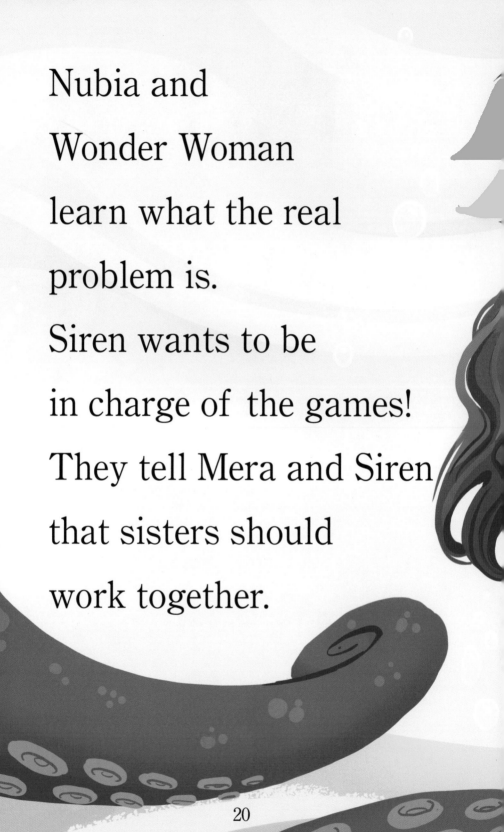

Nubia and
Wonder Woman
learn what the real
problem is.
Siren wants to be
in charge of the games!
They tell Mera and Siren
that sisters should
work together.

Mera is sorry
for not letting
her sister help.
Siren is sorry
for taking over the games.
All the sisters use
their powers to put
everything back together.

Sisters save the day!

Let the games begin!

I LOve you